THE KOOKS: KONK

WISE PUBLICATIONS
PART OF THE MUSIC SALES GROUP
LONDON/NEW YORK/PARIS/SYDNEY/COPENHAGEN/BERLIN/MADRID/TOKYO

PUBLISHED BY
WISE PUBLICATIONS
14-15 BERNERS STREET, LONDON, W1T 3LJ, UK.

EXCLUSIVE DISTRIBUTORS:
MUSIC SALES LIMITED
DISTRIBUTION CENTRE, NEWMARKET ROAD,
BURY ST EDMUNDS, SUFFOLK, IP33 3YB, UK.

MUSIC SALES PTY LIMITED
20 RESOLUTION DRIVE, CARINGBAH,
NSW 2229, AUSTRALIA.

ORDER NO. AM994268
ISBN 978-1-84772-612-4
THIS BOOK © COPYRIGHT 2008 WISE PUBLICATIONS,
A DIVISION OF MUSIC SALES LIMITED.

EDITED BY TOM FARNCOMBE.
MUSIC ARRANGED BY MATT COWE.
MUSIC PROCESSED BY PAUL EWERS MUSIC DESIGN.

PRINTED IN THE EU.

WWW.MUSICSALES.COM

YOUR GUARANTEE OF QUALITY:
AS PUBLISHERS, WE STRIVE TO PRODUCE EVERY BOOK
TO THE HIGHEST COMMERCIAL STANDARDS.

THE BOOK HAS BEEN CAREFULLY DESIGNED TO
MINIMISE AWKWARD PAGE TURNS AND TO MAKE
PLAYING FROM IT A REAL PLEASURE.

PARTICULAR CARE HAS BEEN GIVEN TO SPECIFYING
ACID-FREE, NEUTRAL-SIZED PAPER MADE FROM PULPS
WHICH HAVE NOT BEEN ELEMENTAL CHLORINE BLEACHED.

THIS PULP IS FROM FARMED SUSTAINABLE FORESTS
AND WAS PRODUCED WITH SPECIAL REGARD FOR
THE ENVIRONMENT.

THROUGHOUT, THE PRINTING AND BINDING HAVE
BEEN PLANNED TO ENSURE A STURDY, ATTRACTIVE
PUBLICATION WHICH SHOULD GIVE YEARS OF ENJOYMENT.

IF YOUR COPY FAILS TO MEET OUR HIGH STANDARDS,
PLEASE INFORM US AND WE WILL GLADLY REPLACE IT.

GUITAR TABLATURE EXPLAINED

Guitar music can be notated in three different ways: on a musical stave, in tablature, and in rhythm slashes.

RHYTHM SLASHES: are written above the stave. Strum chords in the rhythm indicated. Round noteheads indicate single notes.

THE MUSICAL STAVE: shows pitches and rhythms and is divided by lines into bars. Pitches are named after the first seven letters of the alphabet.

TABLATURE: graphically represents the guitar fingerboard. Each horizontal line represents a string, and each number represents a fret.

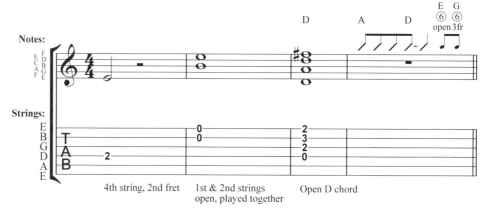

4th string, 2nd fret   1st & 2nd strings open, played together   Open D chord

Definitions for special guitar notation

SEMI-TONE BEND: Strike the note and bend up a semi-tone (½ step).

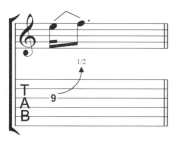

WHOLE-TONE BEND: Strike the note and bend up a whole-tone (full step).

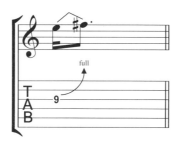

GRACE NOTE BEND: Strike the note and bend as indicated. Play the first note as quickly as possible.

QUARTER-TONE BEND: Strike the note and bend up a ¼ step

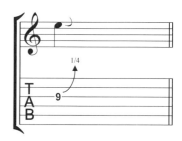

BEND & RELEASE: Strike the note and bend up as indicated, then release back to the original note.

COMPOUND BEND & RELEASE: Strike the note and bend up and down in the rhythm indicated.

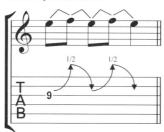

PRE-BEND: Bend the note as indicated, then strike it.

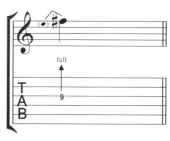

PRE-BEND & RELEASE: Bend the note as indicated. Strike it and release the note back to the original pitch.

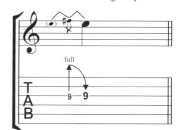

HAMMER-ON: Strike the first note with one finger, then sound the second note (on the same string) with another finger by fretting it without picking.

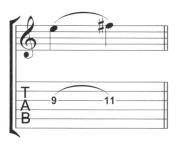

PULL-OFF: Place both fingers on the note to be sounded, strike the first note and without picking, pull the finger off to sound the second note.

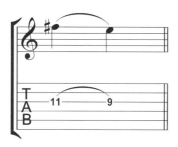

LEGATO SLIDE (GLISS): Strike the first note and then slide the same fret-hand finger up or down to the second note. The second note is not struck.

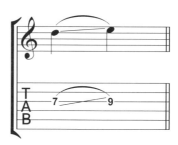

MUFFLED STRINGS: A percussive sound is produced by laying the first hand across the string(s) without depressing, and striking them with the pick hand.

NATURAL HARMONIC: Strike the note while the fret-hand lightly touches the string directly over the fret indicated.

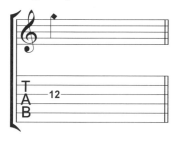

PICK SCRAPE: The edge of the pick is rubbed down (or up) the string, producing a scratchy sound.

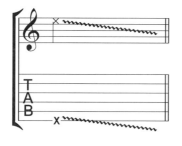

PALM MUTING: The note is partially muted by the pick hand lightly touching the string(s) just before the bridge.

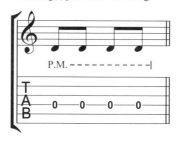

SHIFT SLIDE (GLISS & RESTRIKE) Same as legato slide, except the second note is struck.

TAP HARMONIC: The note is fretted normally and a harmonic is produced by tapping or slapping the fret indicated in brackets (which will be twelve frets higher than the fretted note.)

TAPPING: Hammer ('tap') the fret indicated with the pick-hand index or middle finger and pull-off to the note fretted by the fret hand.

PINCH HARMONIC: The note is fretted normally and a harmonic is produced by adding the edge of the thumb or the tip of the index finger of the pick hand to the normal pick attack.

ARTIFICIAL HARMONIC: The note fretted normally and a harmonic is produced by gently resting the pick hand's index finger directly above the indicated fret (in brackets) while plucking the appropriate string.

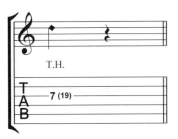
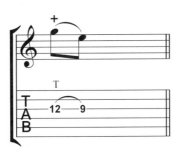
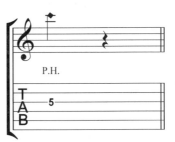
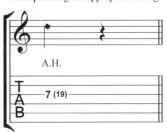

TRILL: Very rapidly alternate between the notes indicated by continuously hammering-on and pulling-off.

RAKE: Drag the pick across the strings with a single motion.

TREMOLO PICKING: The note is picked as rapidly and continously as possible.

ARPEGGIATE: Play the notes of the chord indicated by quickly rolling them from bottom to top.

SWEEP PICKING: Rhythmic downstroke and/or upstroke motion across the strings.

VIBRATO DIVE BAR AND RETURN: The pitch of the note or chord is dropped a specific number of steps (in rhythm) then returned to the original pitch.

VIBRATO BAR SCOOP: Depress the bar just before striking the note, then quickly release the bar.

VIBRATO BAR DIP: Strike the note and then immediately drop a specific number of steps, then release back to the original pitch.

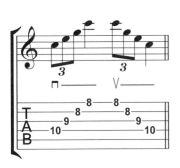
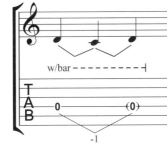

Additional musical definitions

(accent)   Accentuate note (play it louder)

D.S. al Coda

Go back to the sign (𝄋), then play until the bar marked ***To Coda*** ⊕ then skip to the section marked ⊕ ***Coda***

(accent)   Accentuate note with greater intensity

D.C. al Fine

Go back to the beginning of the song and play until the bar marked ***Fine.***

(staccato)   Shorten time value of note

tacet

Instrument is silent (drops out).

⊓   Downstroke

∨   Upstroke

Repeat bars between signs

NOTE: Tablature numbers in brackets mean:
1. The note is sustained, but a new articulation (such as hammer-on or slide) begins
2. A note may be fretted but not necessarily played.

1.   **2.**

When a repeat section has different endings, play the first ending only the first time and the second ending only the second time.

SEE THE SUN

Words & Music by
Luke Pritchard & Paul Garred

†Symbols in parentheses represent names with respect to capoed guitar. Symbols above represent actual sounding chords.
Gtr. 1 tab numbering represents capoed guitar (Tab 0 = 6 fr.).

matter what you do, take a look at yourself and re-a-lise I've been

good to you, I've been good to you.

7

fall,

fall.

Bridge
Gtr. 3 tacet

For all the times___ I ne - ver, ne - ver turned_ a - way,

and now she's here___ on some - one el - se's arm.___

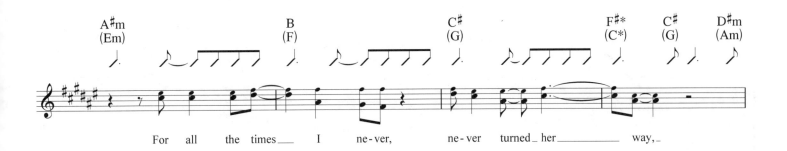

For all the times___ I ne-ver, ne-ver turned_ her_____ way,_

To Coda

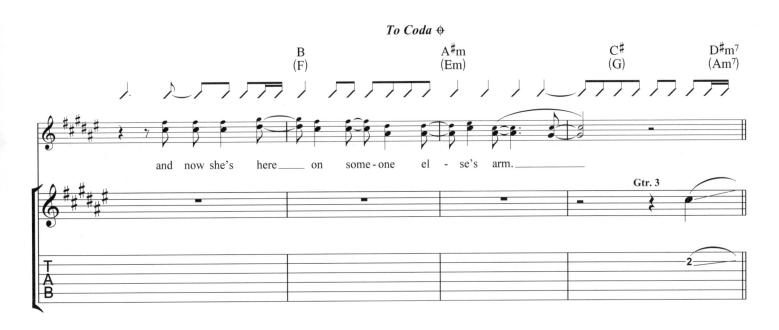

and now she's here_____ on some-one el-se's arm._____

Gtr. 3

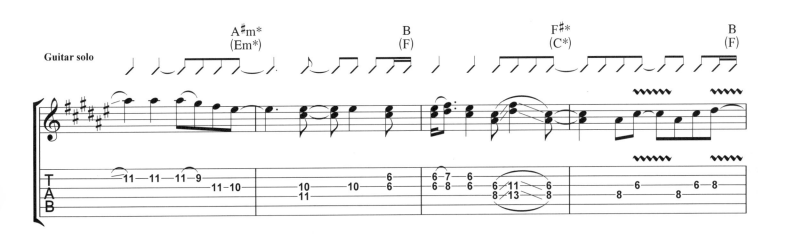

Guitar solo

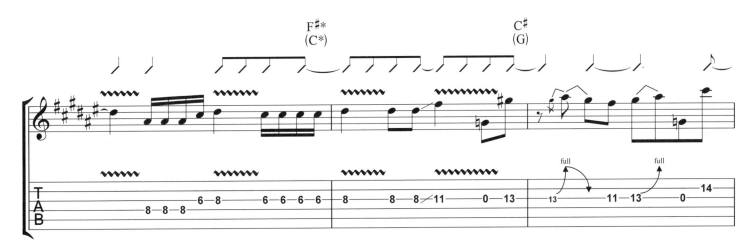

ALWAYS WHERE I NEED TO BE

Words & Music by Luke Pritchard

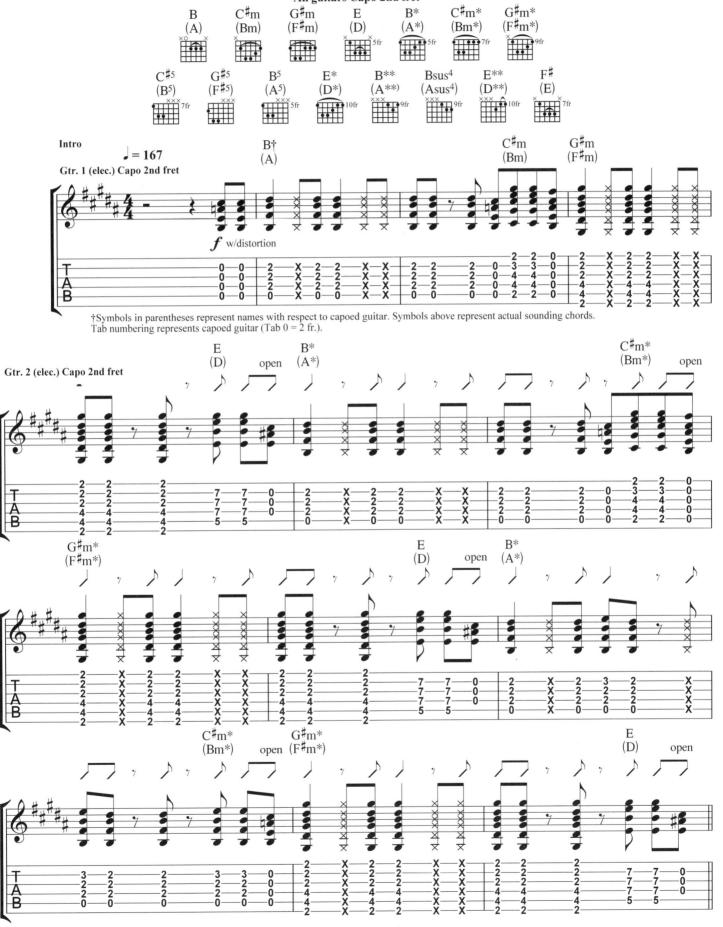

†Symbols in parentheses represent names with respect to capoed guitar. Symbols above represent actual sounding chords.
Tab numbering represents capoed guitar (Tab 0 = 2 fr.).

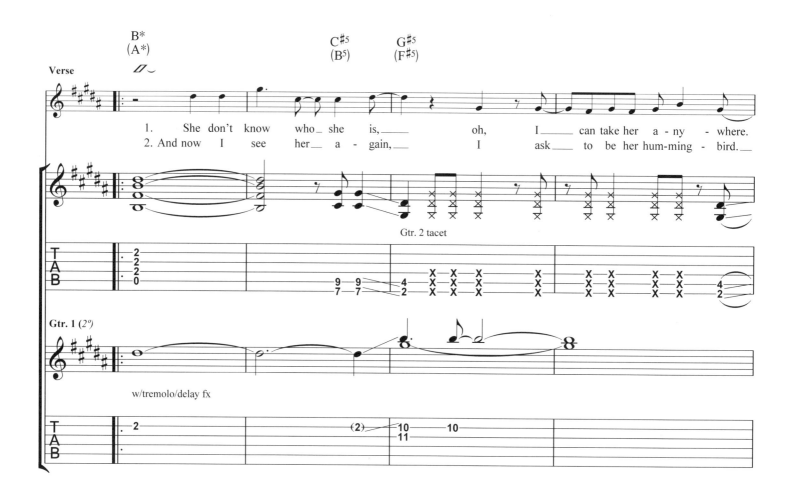

1. She don't know who she is, ___ oh, I ___ can take her a - ny - where.
2. And now I see her a - gain, ___ I ask ___ to be her hum-ming - bird. ___

Do what - ev - er ___ comes nat - 'ral - ly to you, you know she just don't ___
Whis - per words in her ear, ___ oh, now ___ you know I just don't ___

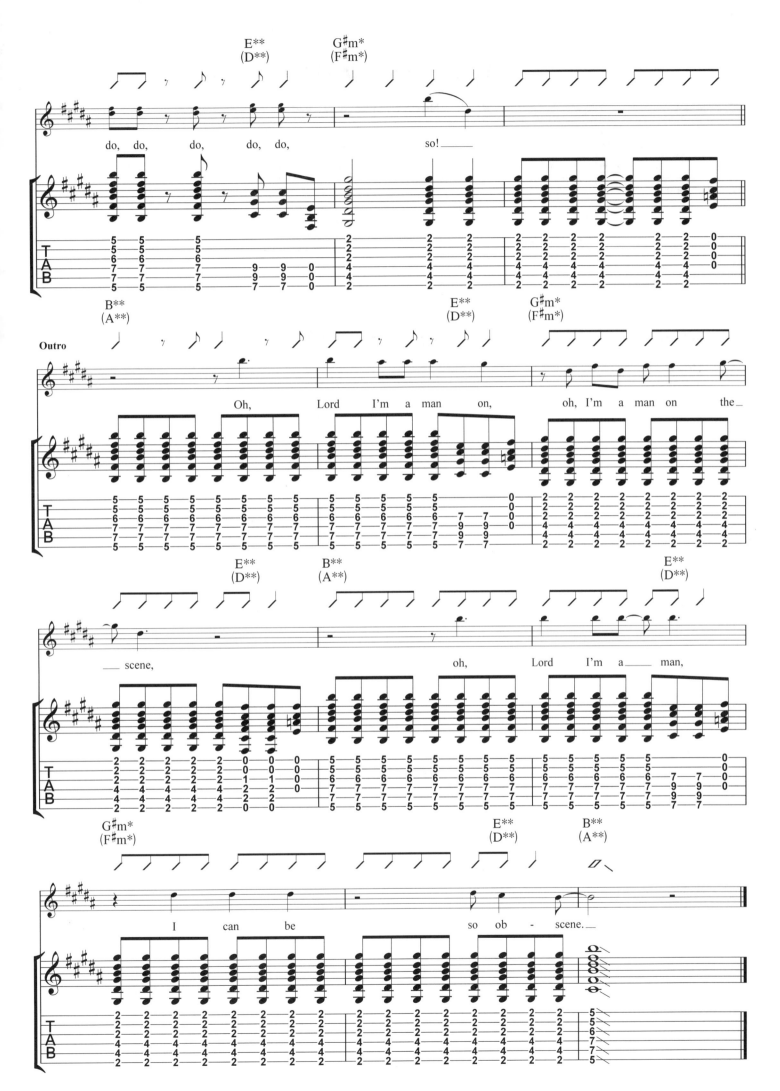

MR. MAKER

Words & Music by Luke Pritchard

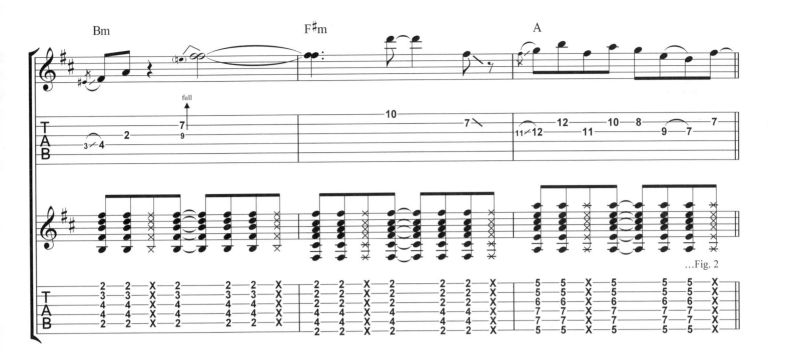

Gtr. 2 plays Fig. 1 *(x4)*

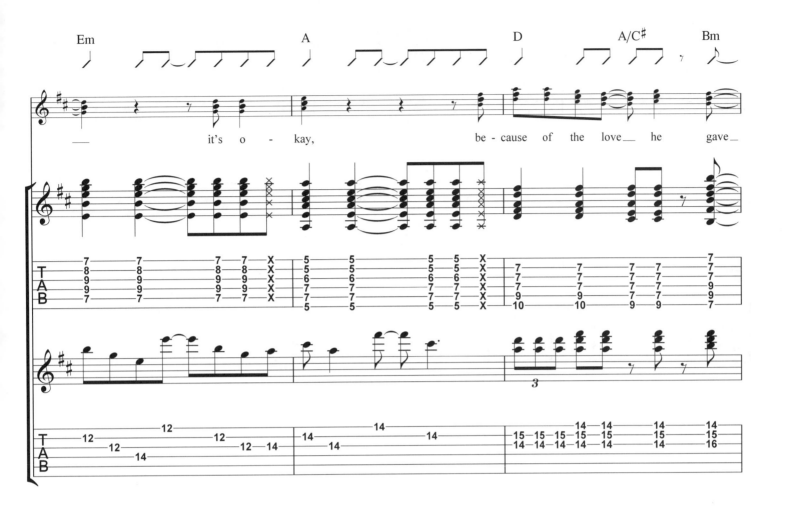

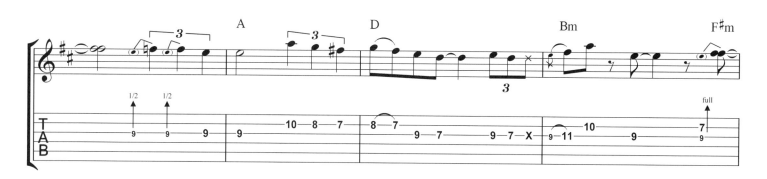

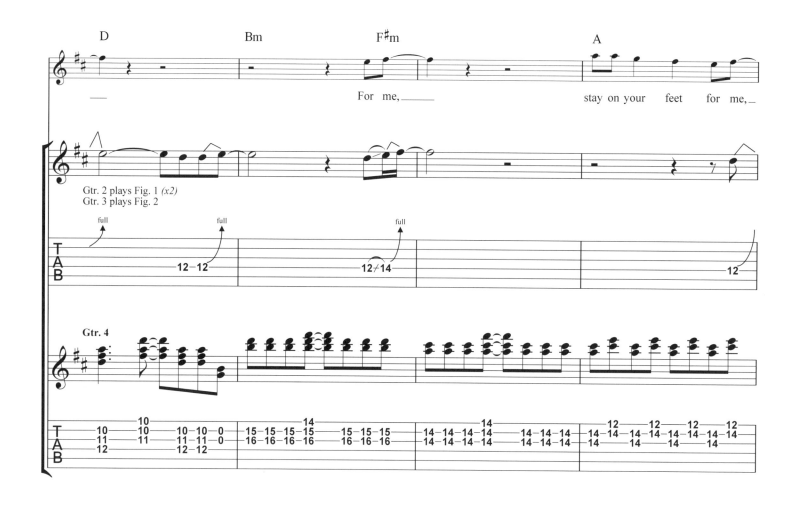

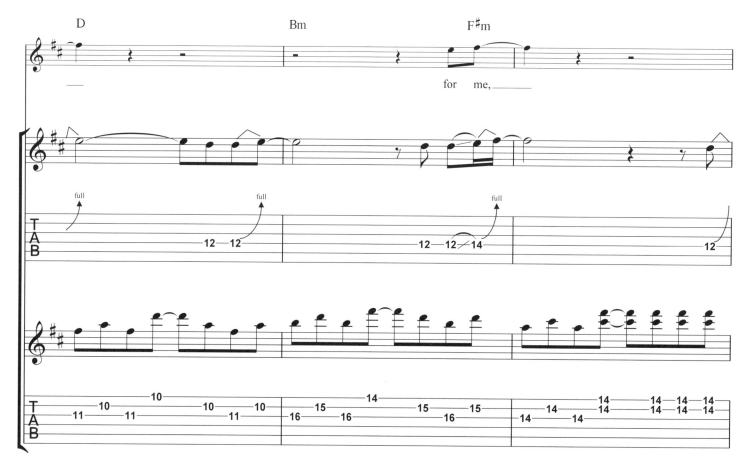

DO YOU WANNA

Words & Music by Luke Pritchard

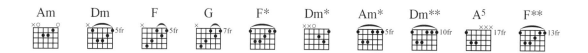

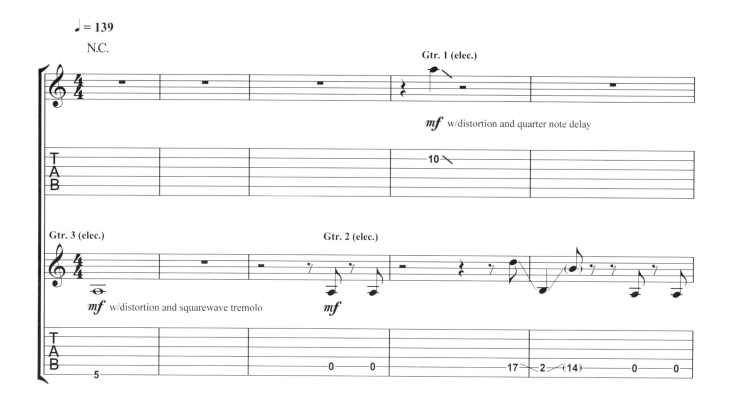

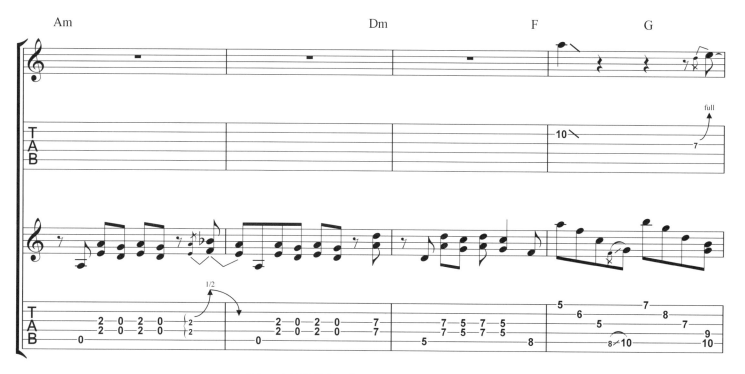

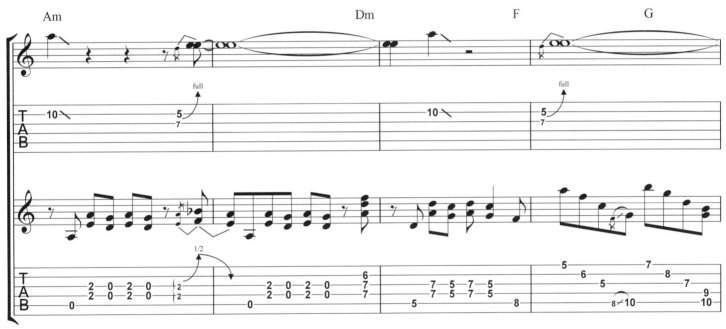

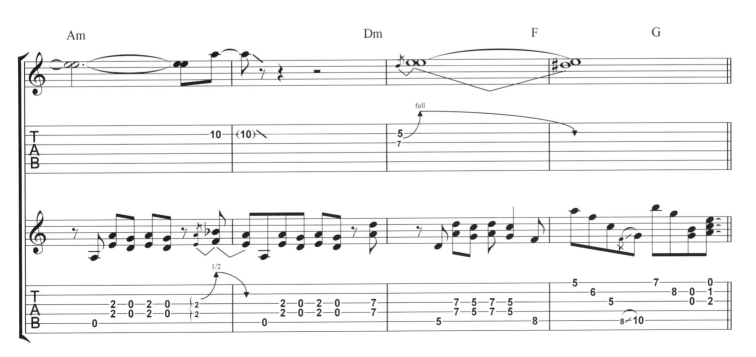

Verse

1. An' I was hop - ing   that you had an at - las in__ your head,_

2. Oh I came to tell you   that you're my fav'- rite girl;__

2° Gtr. 1

Gtr. 3

w/squarewave tremolo

__ so fed up__ of   the same old___ man.

and would you like__ it if__ I   put you in to my world?_

31

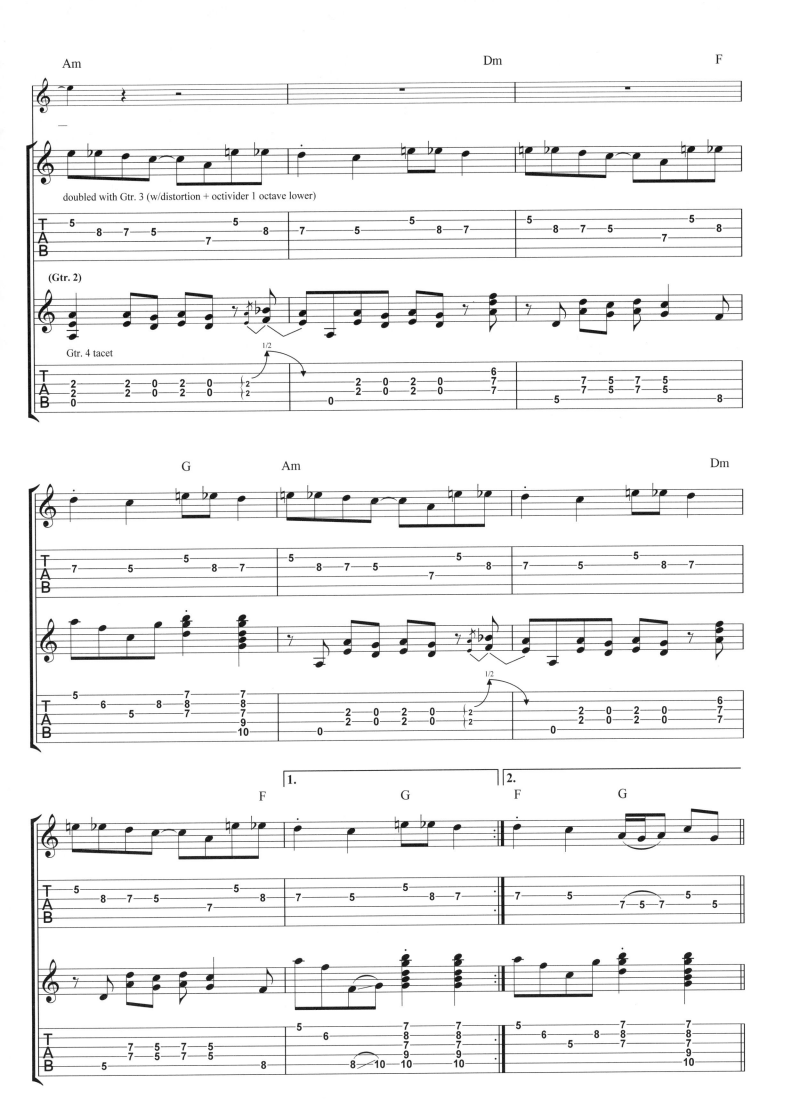

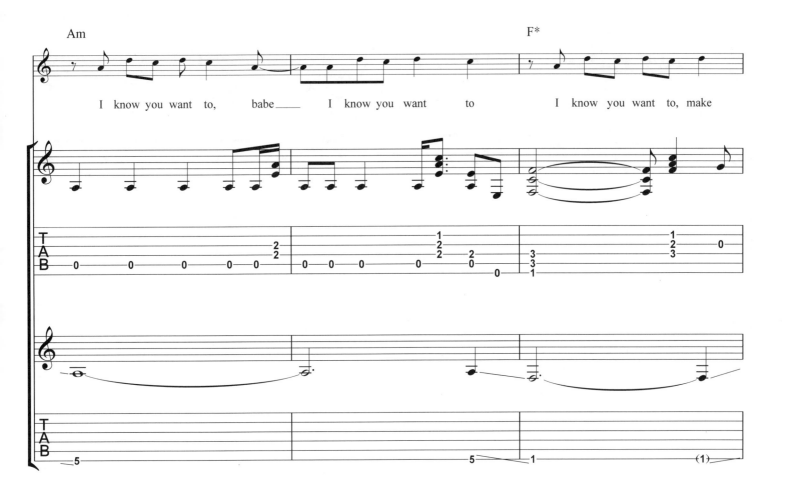

I know you want to, babe___ I know you want to I know you want to, make

love___ to me. Do you wan-na, do you wan-na,

35

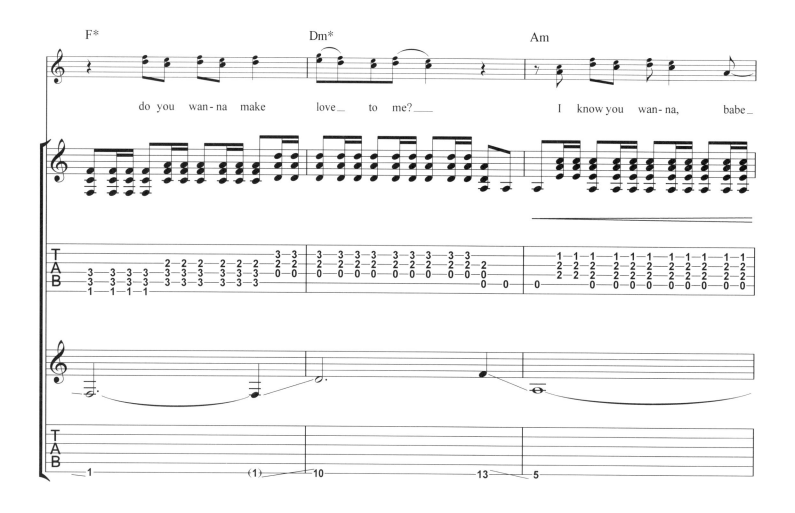

do you wan-na make love__ to me?__ I know you wan-na, babe__

—— I know you wan-na, I know you wan-na make love__ to me.__

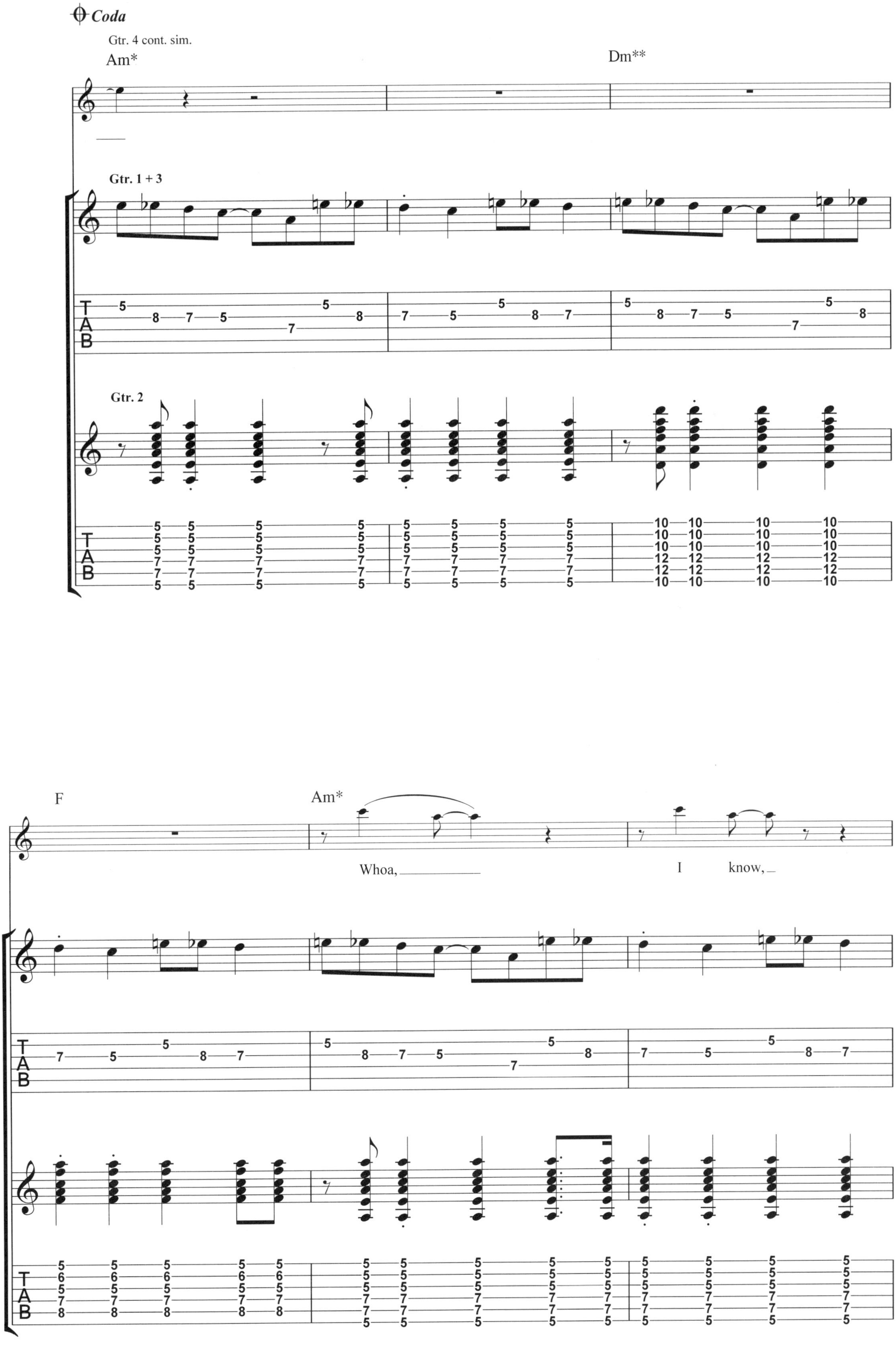
Coda
Gtr. 4 cont. sim.
Am*
Dm**
Gtr. 1 + 3
Gtr. 2
F
Am*
Whoa,
I know,

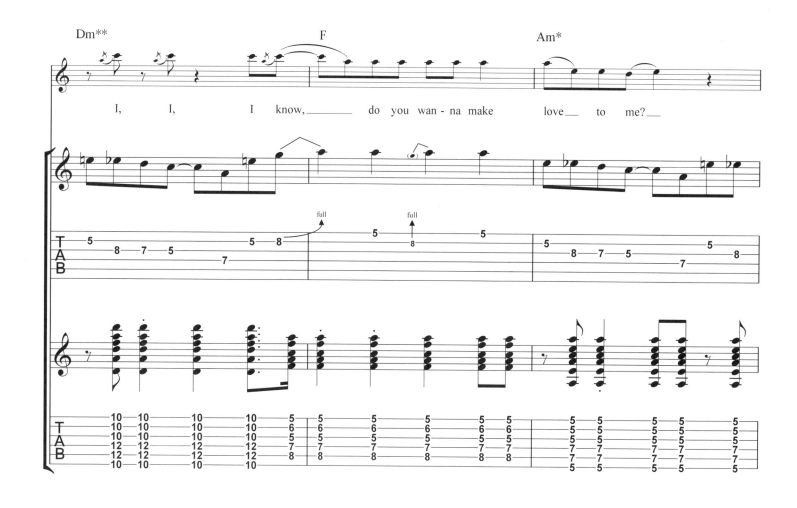

I, I, I know,_____ do you wan - na make love__ to me?__

Make,_ make,_ make. I ___ know, I know you wan - na make

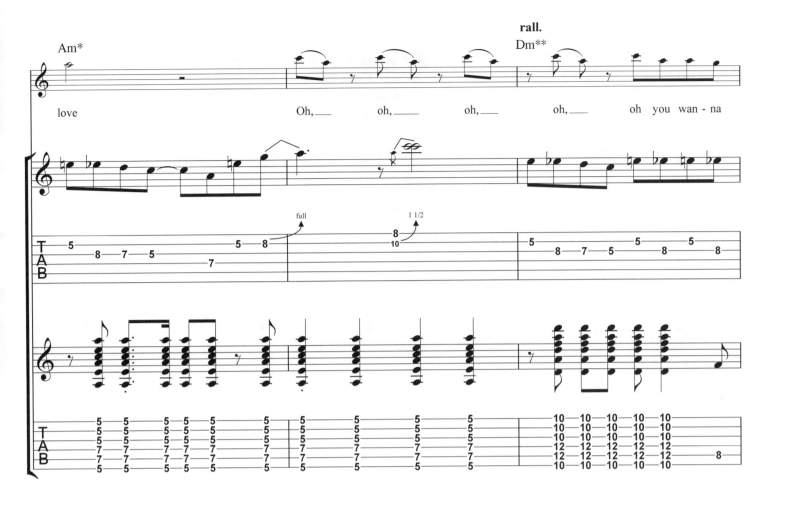

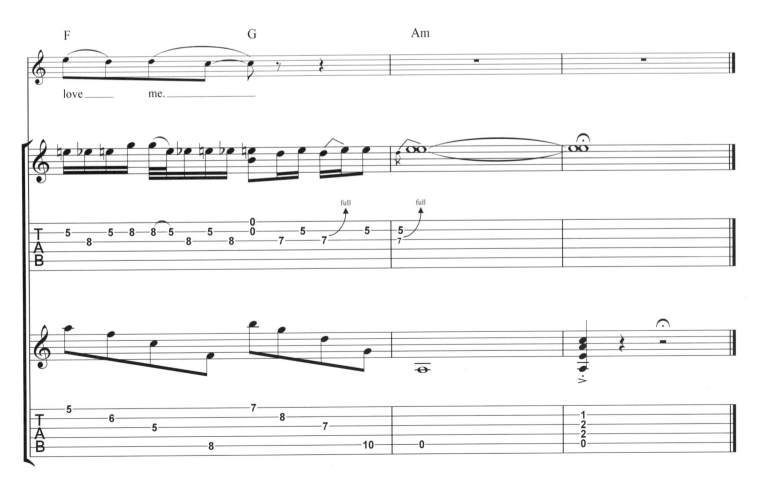

GAP

Words & Music by
Paul Garred, Luke Pritchard & Hugh Harris

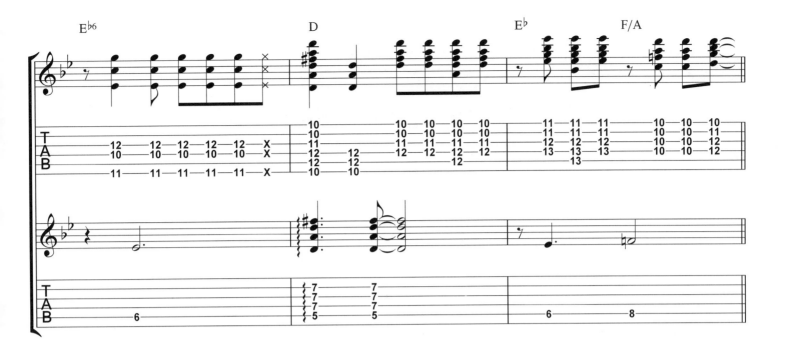

Verse

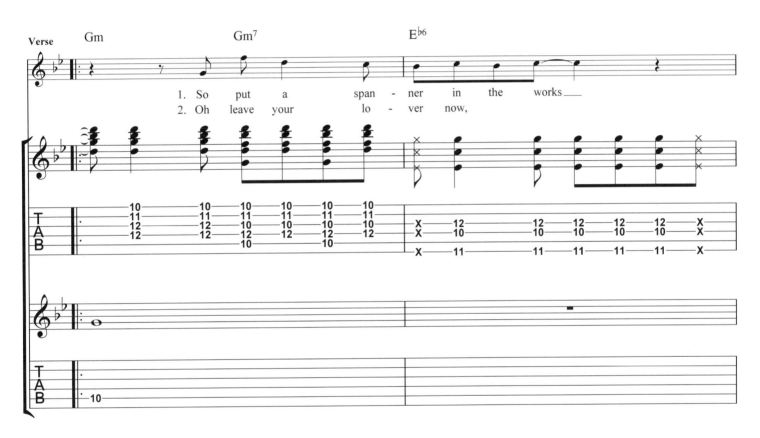

1. So put a span - ner in the works__
2. Oh leave your lo - ver now,

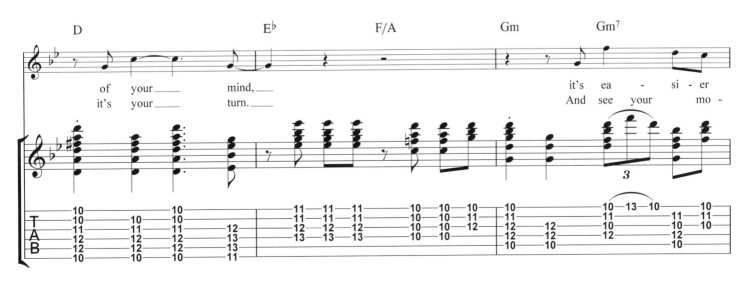

of your__ mind,__ it's ea - si - er
it's your__ turn.__ And see your mo -

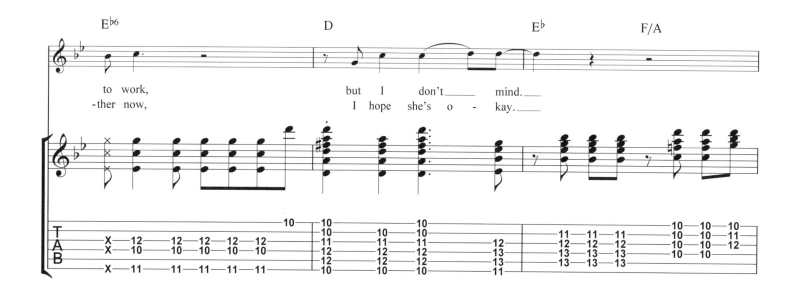

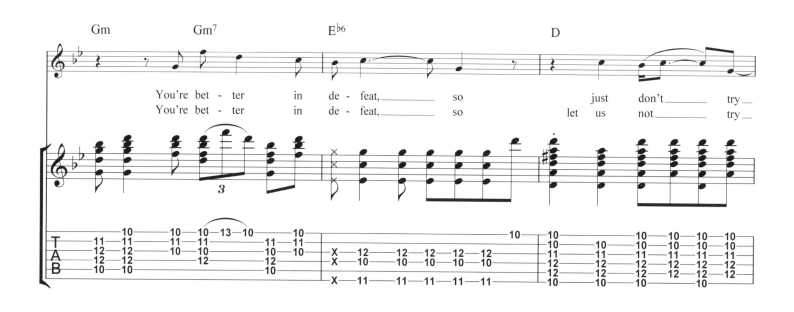

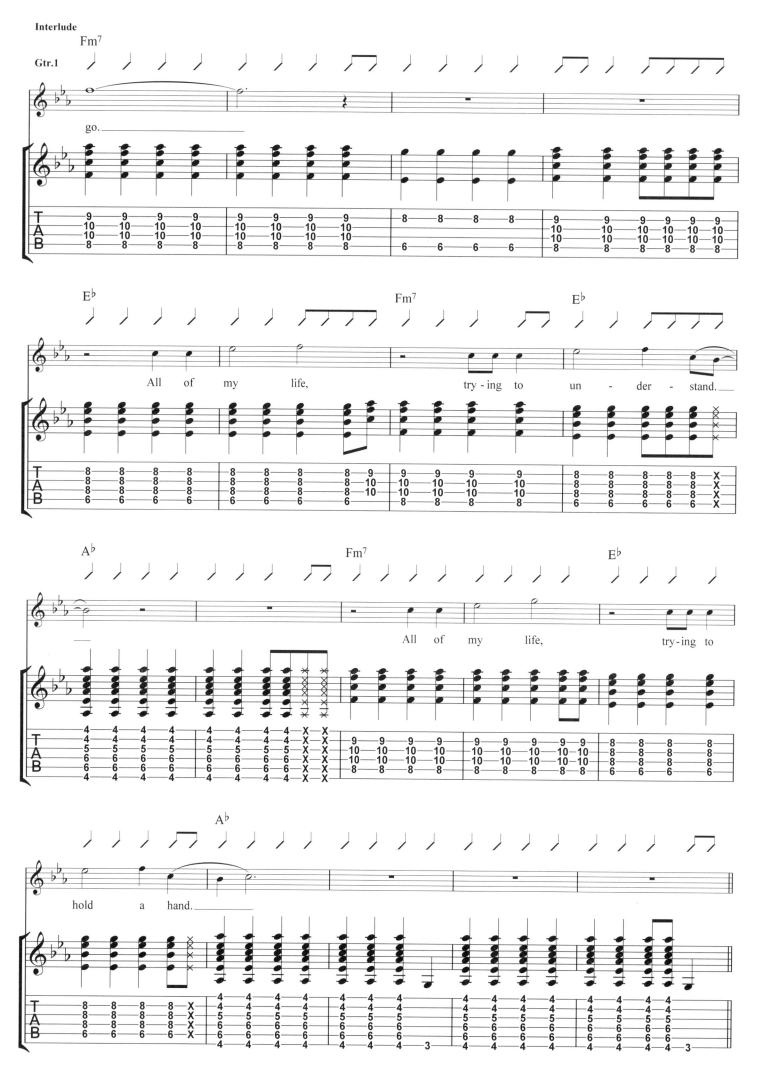

And what's all this___ I see,___ yeah you're leav - ing right___ be - side___

___ me. And I miss___ you and I love___ you and that's___ true.

LOVE IT ALL

Words & Music by
Luke Pritchard & Max Rafferty

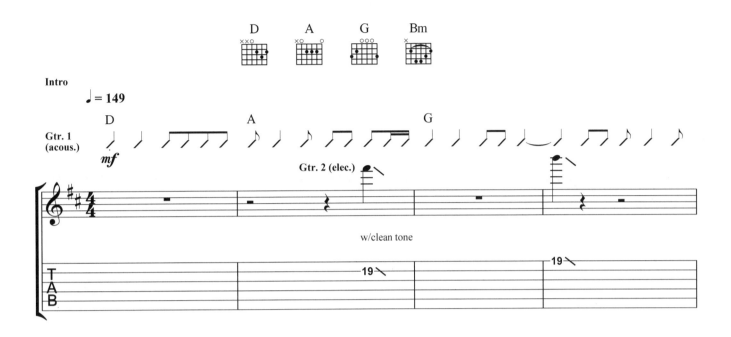

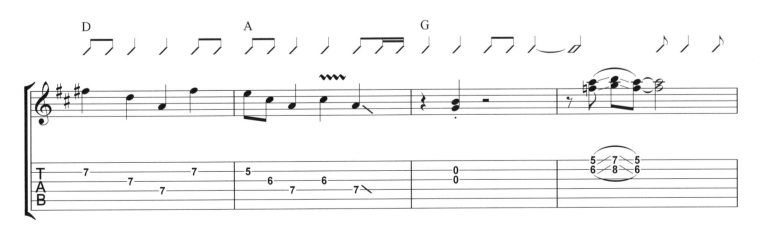

No__ need__ for __ ex - cu - ses,
But on your hand it __ be bro - ken and

and no pres-sures in __ my mind.__
I'll be all o - ver this __ time.__
And she say__

STORMY WEATHER

Words & Music by Luke Pritchard

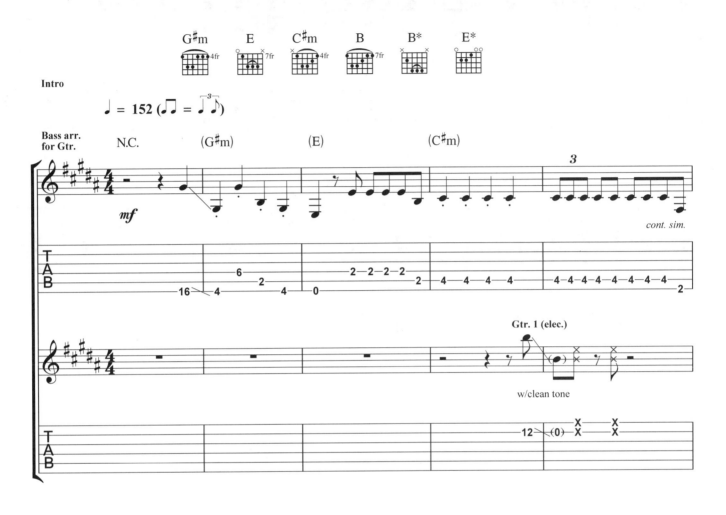

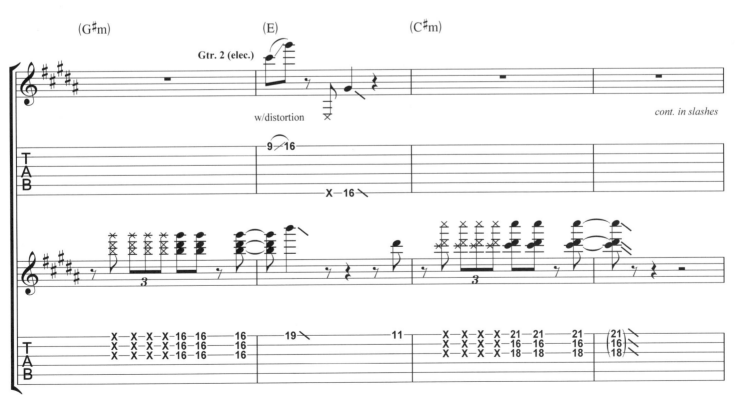

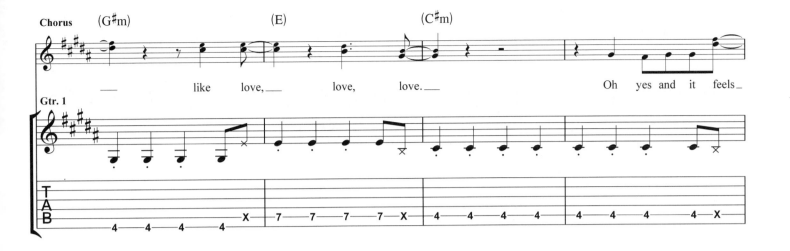

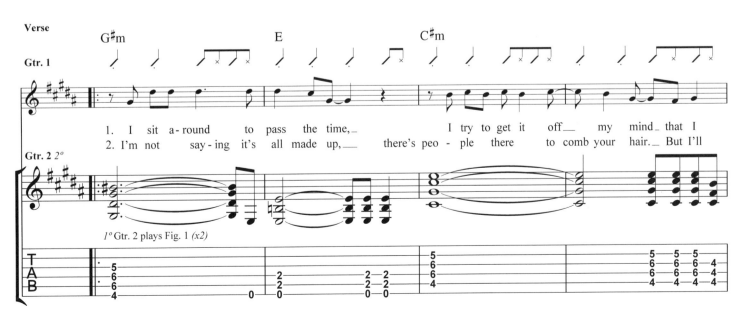

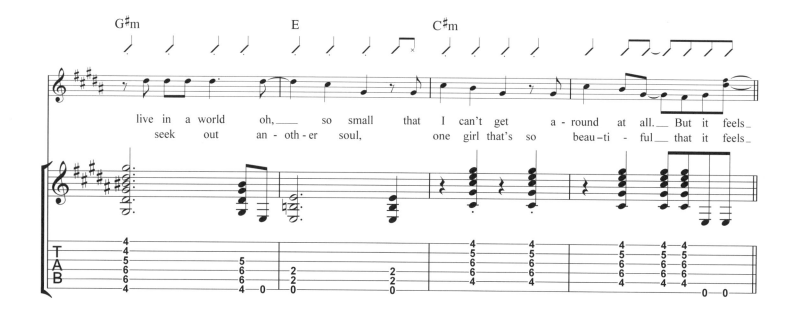

live in a world oh,____ so small that I can't get a - round at all.___ But it feels_
seek out an - oth-er soul, one girl that's so beau -ti - ful___ that it feels_

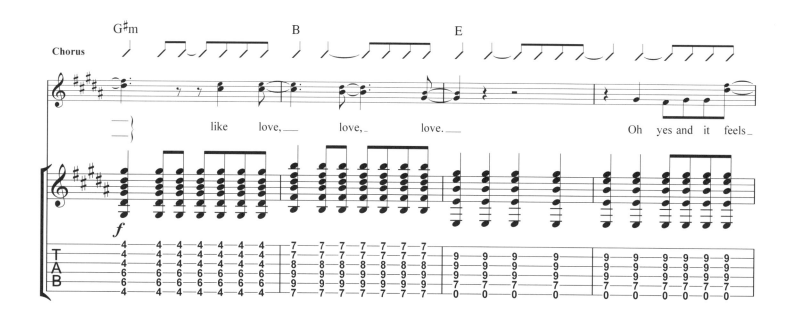

Chorus

like love,____ love,_ love.____ Oh yes and it feels_

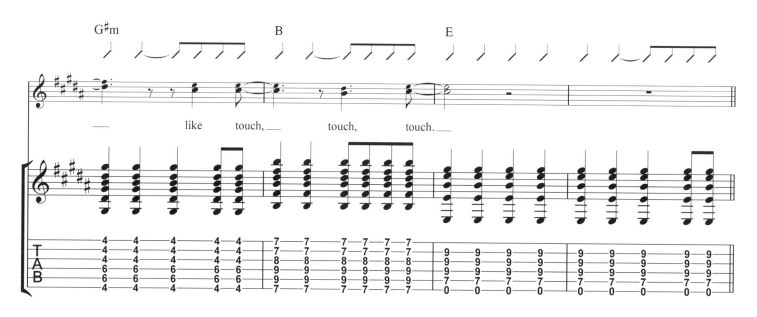

like touch,____ touch,_ touch.____

58

Bridge

What did I say,_____ what did I_____ say,

what did I say?____ Oh,__ I did-n't mean it.____

1.

What did I do,_____ oh, to hurt_____ you? I did-n't

Gtr. 1 *1°*

Gtr. 1 *2°*

mean it,___ oh,___ oh,_ I did-n't mean it.___

And it feels_

SWAY

Words & Music by Luke Pritchard

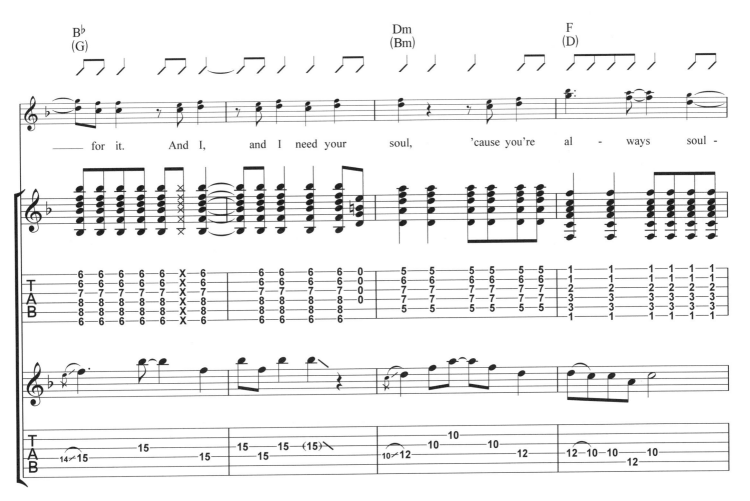

al - ways in the right___ pla - ces.

al - ways___ in the right___ pla - ces.

SHINE ON

Words & Music by Luke Pritchard

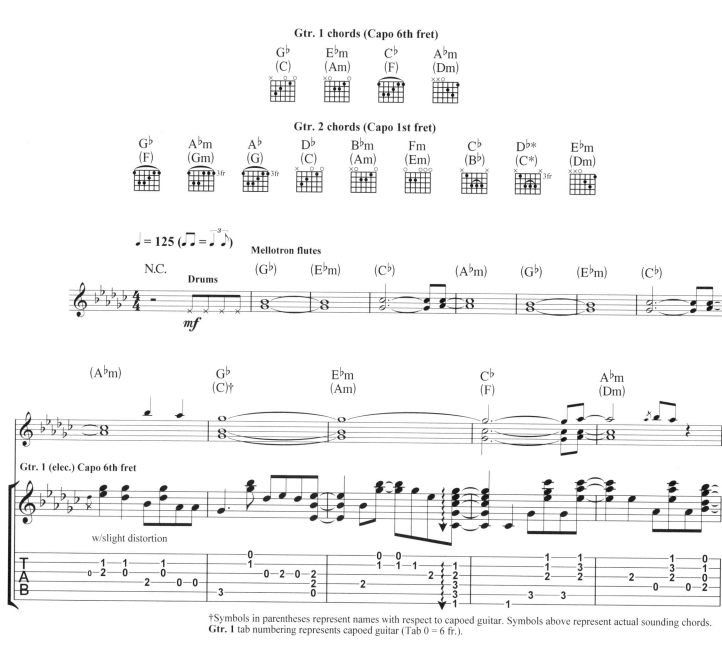

†Symbols in parentheses represent names with respect to capoed guitar. Symbols above represent actual sounding chords.
Gtr. 1 tab numbering represents capoed guitar (Tab 0 = 6 fr.).

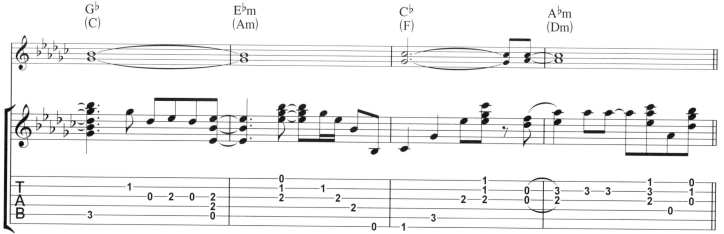

DOWN TO THE MARKET

Words & Music by Luke Pritchard

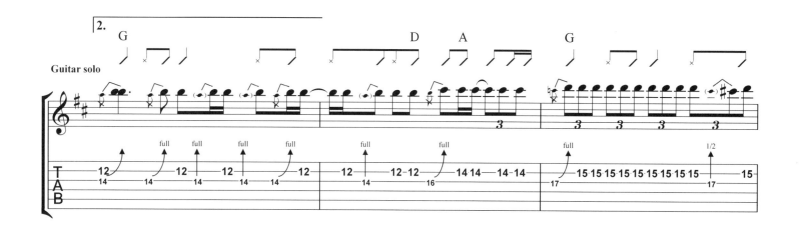

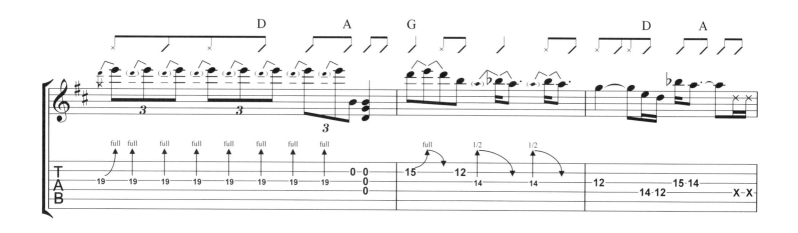

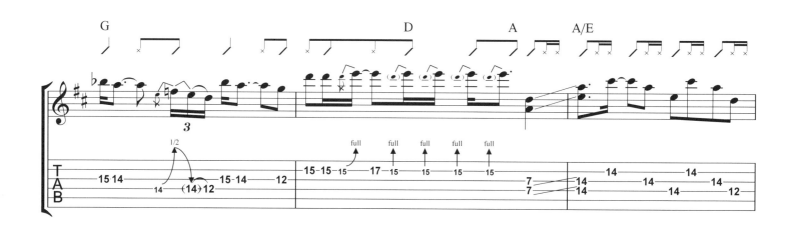

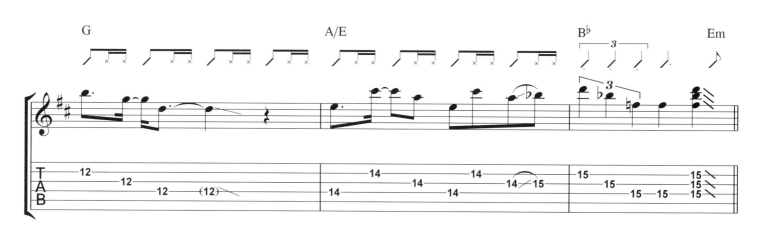

ONE LAST TIME

Words & Music by Luke Pritchard

†Symbols in parentheses represent names with respect to capoed guitar. Symbols above represent actual sounding chords.
Gtr. 1 tab numbering represents capoed guitar (Tab 0 = 6 fr.).

1. Can I hold you one last time?
2. A, B, C, D, E, F and G,
3. Oh, we were lo - vers in ev - 'ry way.

To fight the fear that is
oh, that re - minds me of
Left school to - ge - ther, went

85

TICK OF TIME

Words & Music by Luke Pritchard

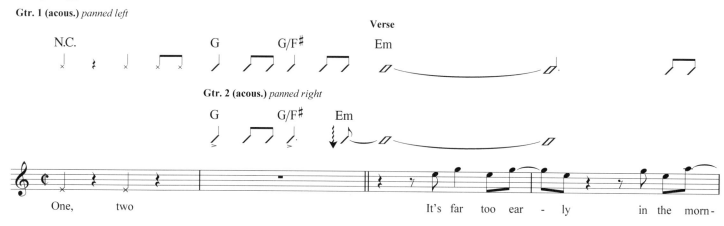

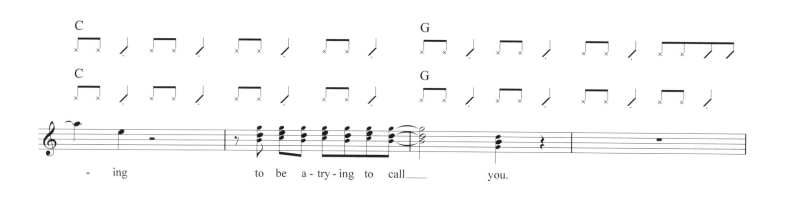

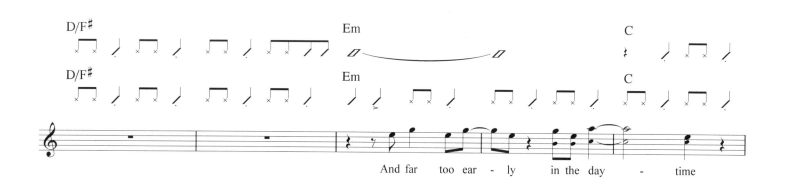

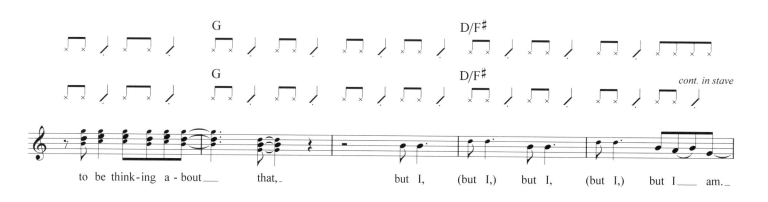

1. What did I do ___ in a past ___ life oh, to de - serve ___
2. What did I do ___ to de - serve ___ her love? I have to ask ___

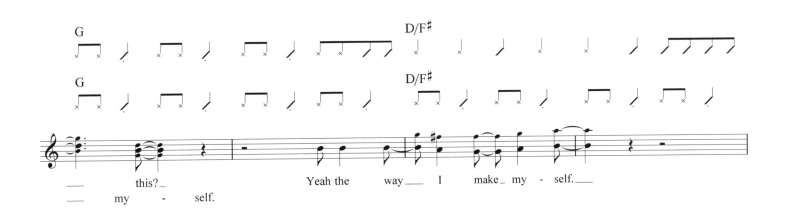

___ this? ___ Yeah the way ___ I make ___ my - self. ___
___ my - self.

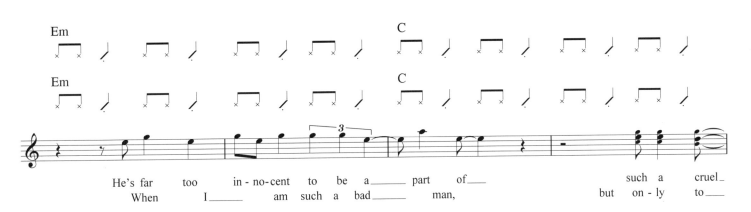

He's far too in - no - cent to be a ___ part of ___ such a cruel ___
When I ___ am such a bad ___ man, but on - ly to ___

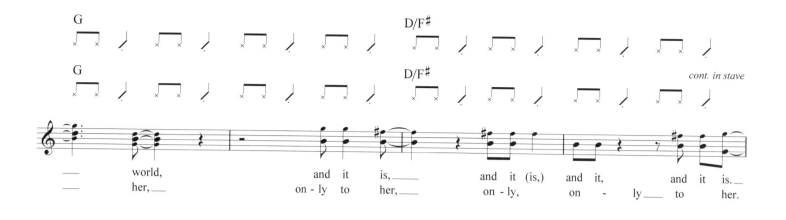

world,　　　and it is,　　　and it (is,) and it,　　and it is.
her,　　　on - ly to her,　　　on - ly, on - ly　to her.

And so I'll　　go,

Chorus

yes I'll　go,　　　so I'll take　that train　　　　and ride.

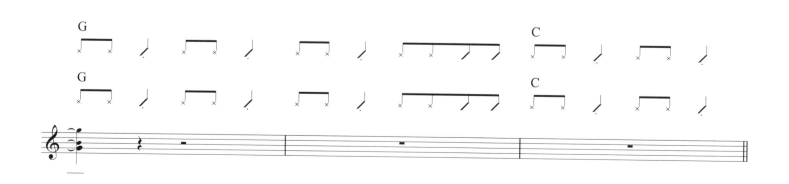

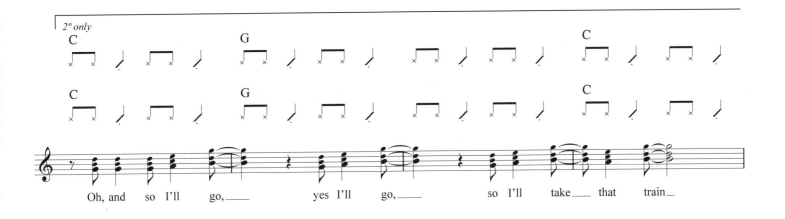

2° only

Oh, and so I'll go,____ yes I'll go,____ so I'll take____ that train____

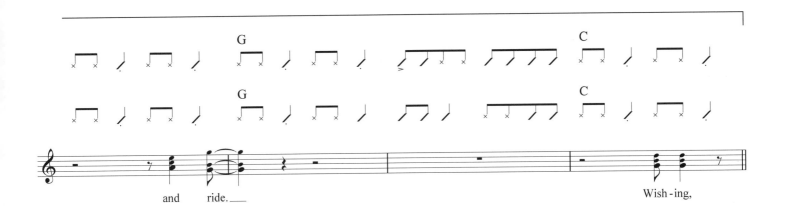

and ride.____ Wish-ing,

Hop - ing I____ could rhyme____ her a rhyme____ that might stop____

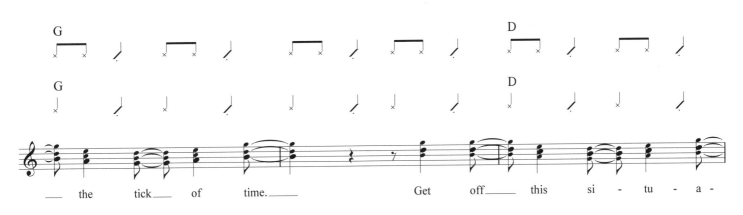

____ the tick____ of time.____ Get off____ this si - tu - a -

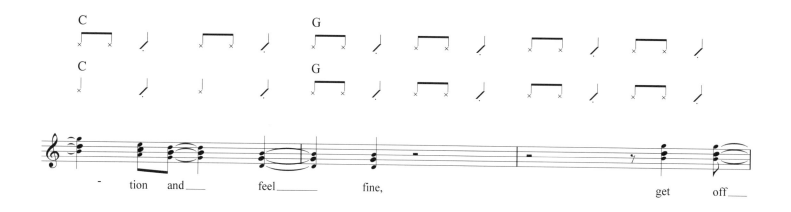

tion and___ feel_____ fine, get off___

1.

___ this si - tu - a - tion and___ feel_____ fine,

2. **rall.**

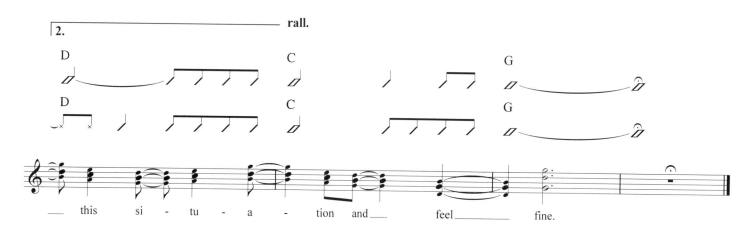

___ this si - tu - a - tion and___ feel_____ fine.

ALL OVER TOWN

Words & Music by Luke Pritchard

Capo 6th fret

†Symbols in parentheses represent names with respect to capoed guitar. Symbols above represent actual sounding chords.
Tab numbering represents capoed guitar (Tab 0 = 6 fr.).

1. Dear___ sir, did I___ see you fleet - ing?
2. What do you see when you see me sir?

I cared for your heart,___ but not___ for it beat - ing.
The ve-ry same thing that makes you bit - ter.